MW01230999

FRIENDLY MONSTERS:

Behind the Computer

BOOKS BY C. PIERRE-RUSSELL

Sheila the Shy Shark

Save the Missing Penny

The Beauty of Love in Those We Shame

Little Kitty Goes to School

Broken before the Storm

The Special Little Sister

The Better Betty

Friendly Monsters: Behind the Computer

Making Dollars Make Sense: Business Ownership at any Age

Butter Me Fly: My Way Home

Publishing Information

Printed in the United States of America

All rights reserved. Except as permitted under the U.S. Copyright Act of 1976, no part of this publication may be reproduced, distributed or transmitted in any form or by any means, or stored in a database or retrieval system, without the prior written permission of the publisher.

This is a work of fiction. The names, dates, places, characters, and incidents are either the product of the author's imagination or are used fictitiously, and any resemblance to actual persons, living or dead, business establishments, events or locales is entirely coincidental and incidental to the real events in the time period in which the story is placed.

Copyright © 2018
Cheurlie Pierre-Russell

Miami, Florida.
All Rights Reserved

Table of Contents

1. The Surprise 5

2. Secrets of the Sand.. 12

3. The Day's End.. 18

4. The Emokee 20

5. A New Day 30

6. Facing the Truth... 33

7. Away with the Fairies... 35

8. Monsters 40

Summary... 49

1
The Surprise

The miserable rain was pouring down again, and Mommy had on her biggest, best hat against it, with a green and yellow flowery raincoat she kept at the very back of her closet, since it didn't rain all that much.

It sure wasn't the best weather for doing what they'd planned— but there was no other day it could be done, was there? Only today! Yes, it all had to be done today, and that was that! No other day would do.

She went to the bottom of the stairs and called up, "Loulou, are you ready yet? Come on, your father's already in the car!"

But there was no answer from upstairs, only the faint sound of Loulou's closet door slamming and the thunder of busy feet in boots she wasn't supposed to put on until she was right by the front door.

The thing was, the whole family was going somewhere special— only, Loulou had no idea where. It was her birthday and a secret mystery drive was what she had asked for as her birthday treat again. They'd done the same thing last year, and the year before that, and the year before that as well! So, what would it be this year? It wouldn't be the zoo. It wouldn't be the fairground. It wouldn't be Crazy Adventure Land.

How did Loulou know all this?

Because these were all the places her parents had taken her to in the years before, that's how!

Loulou was excited, so excited, in fact, that even though she was seven today, she couldn't quite fasten up her coat; she'd missed out a button by mistake so one side trailed low while the other was all twisted and high up off the ground. She hated coats anyway, but Mom had insisted she wear one today. In fact, today was a day for rubber boots and waterproofs—but she really didn't like those either.

She stomped her way down the staircase at long last, her father revving the car just to be awkward and make a point.

"Oh! Lou! You're wearing boots again in the hou—"

Loulou's Mom stopped herself short; today was not the day to start lecturing the little girl about the *no shoes in the house* rule. Nor was she tempted to fix Loulou's coat properly. Today, everything would be just as Loulou wanted it to be.

Loulou shrugged and just grinned broadly while Mom ruffled her girl's unruly hair. "Well, consider yourself lucky it's your birthday," Mom laughed, "Otherwise, you, my girl, would be in deep trouble for those boots!"

Loulou just giggled behind her hand. Mom joined in.

"Come on then, Loopy Lou," Mom said, opening up the front door wide. "You know what your dad's like if we keep him waiting. He'll be like a bear with a sore head."

And Loulou hadn't even had any breakfast yet. What was with all the rush?

Loulou ran outside anyway, her phone grasped firmly in her hand, determined to show all the kids on Facebook how her special day looked; she was going to take pictures and selfies right the way through!

She held up her phone and snapped a quick picture of her father in the driver's seat of the family car, then walked around to the other side and grabbed a close-up shot of her mom's hand as it clasped a bright red handbag. Mom's hand looked *really* pretty in fact; she had just had her nails done and they looked long and shiny, with a purple polish. On her left wrist she wore two bangles, and on one of her fingers sparkled her diamond-studded wedding ring. That would make a brilliant Facebook photo! Loulou's phone snappity-snapped away until Loulou had six photographs of her mom's pretty little hands.

Then Loulou took her seat in the back of the car, sliding her backpack across to the other side. It was kind of weird carrying a backpack when you had no idea where you were going, she thought, so it was almost empty except for her wallet—which only held about $5 anyway—some gum, a hairbrush, and a hair band to keep her frizzy hair in check on the assumption they would be outside, like Mom had said. She opened wide the mouth of the bag and snap-snapped the contents in another photo.

Now she stared down at her big, heavy leather boots with thick soles, photographing those too.

Well, I hope we're not going to a muddy farm, she thought. These boots were old and scruffy but all the kids on Facebook had a pair like them, and nobody else's had pig muck or farmyard mud on them. Well, not that she knew, anyway.

The car set off, Loulou buckling up her seatbelt as it left the driveway while Mom sat in the front, checking a map and trying not to give away the secret of where they were headed. Loulou peered over Mom's shoulder and snapped a picture with her iPhone as Mom quickly snatched the map to one side.

"You'll have to see if the GPS works, Billy," she said to her husband. "*You know who* is peering over my shoulder!"

"Behave yourself!" came the gruff male voice from the driver's seat, aimed at Loulou who sat snickering behind and kicking the back of her father's seat on purpose.

"Aww, spoilsport!" she said as she furtively took a picture of the back of her dad's almost-bald and shiny head with its weird frond of hairs that he used to try and hide the middle bit.

Of course, everyone knew using GPS would have been easier anyhow, but Loulou was sure Mom used a map just so she could pretend to hide their route and make a show of lowering the volume every time Loulou tried to see. Loulou managed to get a quick video of her mom's swift hand movements with the phone showing the GPS direction.

As she settled back against the leather seat, Loulou fiddled about with her iPhone, logging into her Facebook page and uploading the photos with a little commentary for each one, a few words she thought up carefully.

This was just so cool! By the end of the day, she was sure she would have loads of Likes on all her uploads. Maybe even more Likes and hearts than she could count! And she couldn't wait to see all the funny emojis her friends would use and how jealous they'd be of her special day.

Now, Loulou smiled and rested her big fuzzy hairdo against the back seat and dozed off; as usual, she'd stayed up too late the night before, so it wasn't the best start to the day.

She was soon away in dreamland.

2
Secrets of the Sand

*L*oulou..." came the distant voice. "Lou, wake up, we're here!"

Mom held the car door open and was poking at Loulou gently with one manicured fingertip, shaking her shoulder and speaking into her ear. That really took quite some effort because nobody could even see where Loulou's ears were through the mop of red hair. Loulou's eyes opened quickly and she saw her father standing ahead of the car, getting a parking ticket from a meter.

On one side, she could only see the street filled with little boutiques selling clothing and candy and things for the beach. On the other, she saw a scene that made her eyes grow wide and round, with little silvery sparkles of excitement dancing in them, and crinkles at the corners from her big smile.

Look!

They were right by the sand! Loulou's parents had taken her to the sea; Mom was already waving at an ice-cream seller, making sure he didn't close up his small booth before she had bought them all a Super Whippy Ice with colored sprinkles on the top. "Come on!" Mom said again.

"Wait a minute," said Loulou. "I need a picture..."

Mom wasn't sure what Loulou could possibly want a photo of now—it was already proving pretty hard to get through a normal day with a kid who just had to take a snapshot of everything and post it to Facebook! But she didn't really mind; this was Loulou's special day, after all.

And it had only been in the last year that Loulou had even been allowed to use Facebook, so it was still kind of new and fun. Mom and Dad thought Loulou was really too young for Facebook but they'd eventually decided she could have her own page as long as they had access to it too—after all, all the other kids had a page of their own and they didn't want her to be left out. Her parents knew it must be hard enough being the ginger-haired kid at a new school; they had to let her belong to the in-crowd or they were sure she could end up bullied.

Loulou snapped an image of her mom hanging onto the car door, the wild wind whipping Mom's hair into a frenzy and blowing her raincoat inside out. Mom held a baby-blue umbrella in her other hand and clutched a small folding seat under her arm.

Click click! Clickety-click!

She clicked 'send', and off the picture went—*zoooooooom*, like a miniature flash of lightning—landing on Loulou's Facebook page with the comment, "This is my mom. She's ready for anything!"

The truth was, Loulou adored her mom. She was kind and gentle, and generous, and kissy-kissy and huggy, and she was also very, very pretty. Oh, and she was smart, too!

The family walked hand in hand, aiming toward the beach. Loulou thought it smelled of the fresh but salty sea air and slimy green seaweed, and of clawed crabs and pink and white candyfloss, and of toasted s'mores.

They crossed a little sidewalk covered in dusty sand and reached the edge of the beach where wet sand trailed down to the water's edge.

"Stop!" she cried out, all of a sudden. She rummaged in her coat pocket and brought out her phone again.

Snap-snap! Snap-snap! SNAP!

Her parents walked on ahead, Dad's hair waving all over in the breeze; it was what some would call a *comb-over*, a big floppy piece of gray hair flap-flapping across his bald and shiny head. It seemed to dance in the wind, as if celebrating Loulou's birthday in time to a drum beat nobody could hear because that, too, had been kept a secret for Loulou's special day.

Dad's pants flapped about in the wind too. He didn't even own a pair of beach shorts, but even if he'd had a pair, it was probably too chilly for them today. And anyway, Loulou didn't really want to see her father's knobbly white knees and his hairy legs!

Loulou's mom pulled the collar of her raincoat in tighter but the back of it still blew and billowed about, making Loulou laugh loudly.

Snap-snap went Loulou's camera app. Then she huddled up inside her coat, facing away from the cutting wind, tapping away at her phone screen to get the photo sent to Facebook. She imagined all her friends giving her picture the big thumbs-up and a million— no, a trillion!—Likes.

"Go, girl!" they'd say, and "Wow, your mom is so pretty!" Or even, "Love your mom's raincoat, Lou! She's so stylish!"

Down on the foreshore, the threesome stooped and crouched by tiny rockpools, seeking out the hermit crabs they knew were hiding there. They were as close as peas in a pod. Loulou loved her mom and dad so very much. How many other little girls had parents who'd get out of bed early, fill the car with gasoline and drive for three hours to take their birthday girl to a windy, rainy beach? She felt so happy and proud.

They spent a full hour down on the sand, the waves crashing up onto the shore and coming closer and closer, and seabirds floating high overhead. A vicious storm was going to come in, Loulou could sense it and see it in the black clouds, so she pointed at the sky.

"Mom, look at that!" she said. "It's like God is angry at me."

Her mother turned and put a loving arm around Loulou's shoulder, pulling her in close to her own body in a tight hug.

"Silly girl," she said, into the wind. "God is never going to be angry, not with you, anyway. You are my perfect girl, always will be."

Mom then added something else.

"Why don't you take pictures of the sky? And the crashing waves? Your friends would love to see them!"

Loulou thought about it. "I don't think so, Mom," she answered. "My friends aren't really into nature shots, you know?"

And with that, as if it was the most beautiful thing she had ever seen in her short life, Loulou looked down and snapped a photo of a black and white soccer ball some other kid must have left on the beach: *Adidas* it said on one side.

"That's what the kids like, Mom!" she said. She was careful to get her own boots into the shot too, just as if she was going to kick the soccer ball. And then she clicked *send*.

Loulou's mom turned to her now, her own silver iPhone in her hand. "Lou," she said, "Go sit on that rock, there, while I get a photograph of you."

Loulou did as she was told.

"You won't put that on Facebook, will you?" she asked. "And don't send it to anyone."

Mom just laughed. "Come on," she said. "We'd better catch up with Dad—looks as if he's heading for those Super Whippy Ices."

3
The Day's End

The day gradually drew to a close, but Loulou was so very happy. They'd done everything there was to do down by the sea. They'd eaten ice cream, played ball, chased after a silly lost dog, scoured the pools for fish and crabs, and eaten ham sandwiches Mom had carefully prepared at home before they'd left. They tasted extra scrumptious in the open air and the wind and the rain. Even if it was a wet day, Loulou couldn't have enjoyed it more.

Loulou's special boots were muddy from the oily foreshore, and sand had gotten in the tops, making her feet sore on the heels. She craved a hot shower. But for now, right this minute, a lemonade and a sticky bun would certainly do!

They sat in the beachside café, where warm air blasted through the big blowers mounted high on the ceiling. Loulou could feel her aching bones drying out and she wondered if this was how it felt to be a piece of wet laundry hung on a clothesline to dry.

Dad had a large latte and Mom had a pot of tea. Mom's hand against the white mug looked super special again, her bangles and gold ring glistening in the lights from above. Once, on TV, Loulou had seen a program about a woman who'd earned lots and lots of money because she had such pretty hands and she turned into a hand model—getting paid to do advertisements for jewelry and nail polish and all sorts of things. Can you believe that?

Well, anyway, when Loulou posted a photo of her mom's hands curled around her white mug in the café, she put a caption:

"Mom could be a hand model!"

Then she forgot all about it.

It was time they started on their way home. Loulou couldn't wait to get in through their front door and to see all her trillions of *Likes*, all the super emojis and the comments about her wonderful day. She was so excited, she was the very first to jump down from her chair and say, "Come on! We have to get back home!"

Mom and Dad began to wonder what on earth was wrong with her, wanting to go home when she usually put up a good argument for staying out longer.

But they were not going to fight about it—they were secretly thrilled—so they pushed their plates and cups into the middle of the table, got up, and herded Loulou toward the door to the street. Then, it'd be just a very short walk back to their waiting car.

Loulou had such an amazing day. What lovely parents she had! She thought she was very blessed and that today, God had been extra good to them all.

4
The Emokee

The family sat around the dinner table at home. Everything in the house had looked just the same as normal when they'd arrived back, as if that amazing day at the beach hadn't happened at all!

That lazy, slobbery old dog was still curled in his bed in the hallway, snoring.

The laundry basket still looked full to bursting in the upstairs bathroom.

Loulou's closet door was still wide open and all her clothes still spilling out across the floor and the bed, just as she'd left them.

That was the funny thing about real life; things didn't just change while you were out of the house; you had to make things change yourself. And this was what made Facebook so much fun for a seven-year-old girl! On Facebook, just about anything could be posted or said while you were out for the day!

Loulou shuffled in her chair, anxious to get away from the dining table and check on what everyone had written in response to all her posts during the birthday at the beach. "Mom?" she asked, playing with her dessert spoon.

"Yes, sweetie?"

"Please may I leave the table?"

"Well, you can, but are you sure? You haven't had any pudding! You don't want any today? You're not sick, are you?" Mom asked, looking a little anxious.

"No Mom, I'm not sick, I just don't want pudding. Maybe later…" Loulou said, swinging her feet under the table.

"Okay, well, off you go then."

Loulou's father pushed his black-rimmed eyeglasses right down onto the tip of his nose and peered over them at his wife after Loulou had gone.

"Well, you know what she's doing right now, don't you?" he asked.

"No, what?"

"Come on. Sure, you know. It begins with F."

Loulou's mom looked a little quizzical for a moment, then her face broke into a crooked smile. "Oh! That!" she said. "Facebook?"

"You got it," Dad said, shaking his head. "You don't think it's turning into an addiction? I mean, she's on that thing all the time. I'm surprised she hasn't turned into an emokee."

"A what?"

"You know, an emo—thing, whatever the word is," he said, hesitant.

"Emoji. Like a smiley face," Mom said.

"That's the one. Just what I said, an emokee."

They laughed together, and Dad thought it was so funny, some of his drink of tea shot down his nose. He grabbed his napkin and dabbed at his face. "Whoops," he said. "Pardon me."

They laughed again.

But then they stopped laughing.

The room grew quiet and still, the air even seeming a little chilly all of a sudden. Loulou had appeared in the doorway, clutching her laptop. Her face was streaked with tears and her eyes were all red from crying.

Mom jumped to her feet and rushed over to Loulou, putting a gentle arm around her neck. "Oh, sweetheart!" she cried. "What's the matter? You were fine when you went upstairs. You can't cry on your birthday."

She ushered Loulou back to the table where Dad also rose and ruffled his daughter's fluffy big red mop of hair.

Loulou could barely speak, and her little shoulders shook as she sobbed. She placed her laptop down on the dining table and opened it up to show her Facebook page to her parents. Mom and Dad peered in close. They could see Loulou's photo gallery with all the day's beautiful images: the trip in the car; Dad's shining head from behind as he drove; Mom clutching onto her red purse; the sand down on the beach; the pictures from the café; the crabs and sea snails and rock pools; and many, many more.

Mom glanced at the one where she held onto her red purse. There were only two Likes and one heart, and all of these were from family members. Aunt Hattie, Grandma, and cousin Alison had been the only ones to leave nice comments.

"Looks like you're off somewhere real smart!" Aunt Hattie had posted.

"Have a wonderful birthday, Loopy!" said Grandma.

Cousin Alison had posted, "I wish I could go with you. XXXX"

Underneath all these comments were more words though, words that blurred Loulou's vision and bit at her skin with salty tears. "That purse looks like it came from Walmart," one girl from school had commented. "Looks plastic to me."

"Who still drives a car like that? You should see what *my* dad drives!" said another, posting a picture of a huge black sedan with tinted windows, the sort that really important people drove around in.

"Your mom's nails make her look like a witch," went another.

Dad peered in at the comments about his hair.

"Your dad wears a wig, hahahaha," said the first.

"No, he doesn't," said the comment underneath that one. "Nothing could stick on that shiny head. It's like a skating rink! *My* dad's got lots and lots of hair."

Someone else posted, "Careful traveling right behind your dad like that. His hair might fly off and choke you."

Loulou pointed to the picture from the café, the one where her Mom held onto the coffee mug. "Ewww!" one comment said. "Your mom wears fake diamonds—even a kid wouldn't wear those."

And so it went on, and on, and on. Finally, someone Loulou didn't even know, chimed in, trying to defend her. But even that comment turned out bad. "Just because her family's really poor, don't be mean," the girl said.

Poor? *Was* Loulou's family really poor? She had not ever thought about it. But now she did, maybe it was true. Mom had not worked for years, not since she'd been sick with stress and eventually lost her job.

Loulou's dad just worked part-time in an engineering firm, cleaning up the factory floors and refilling the boxes of machine parts. She'd never realized any of that mattered before. Mom and Dad were always there for Loulou, night or day, whenever she needed them for anything.

Dad always helped Loulou with her homework and even lent her a hand when she had to do chores; Mom was always giving out extra pocket money because Loulou did her chores so well while Mom was out at the store buying groceries. She'd never known it was mostly Dad who did the work, and not Loulou!

"Shh," Dad had always said to Loulou. "It all gets done faster if I do them too." And then he would slip her an extra coin for all the chores she hadn't done.

Mom, though, was the one who always was there to give out cuddles when Loulou was upset—like now—or who tucked Loulou into bed when she wasn't feeling well, perching herself on the bed corner to make funny faces at her girl until she smiled again.

Dad was the one who drove Loulou everywhere, even to the places neither of them ever wanted to go—like the dentist or the hospital.

And Mom was the one who always made sure that there was good and healthy food on the table for them all, every single night of the week. "To make you big and strong and brainy!" she'd say. "Here, Loulou; you get more pie, to make you big and strong." Or, "Have more carrots, my Loopy Lou. They give you that lovely hair."

And about Loulou's hair; well, one girl from school had even picked on that in the photo comments.

"Her hair looks like a beetle's nest!"

"Yuk!" said another. "Maybe beetles *and* snakes in that."

Loulou couldn't stop crying and her heart was broken in bits. Mom felt as if someone had pushed *her* over in the playground too; she remembered how it had felt to be the bullied girl at a new school.

When Loulou's mom had been growing up, there had been a girl at school who must have been just like these on Loulou's Facebook page. She was called Julie; Unruly Julie, the headmistress had called the girl. That was many, many years ago—and it was something she had tried to forget and leave in her past. But at times like this, Unruly Julie came bullying her way back into Mom's thoughts.

"Lou," she said, softly. "You know there are girls—and boys— like these all over the world. And you know what?"

Loulou looked up under glistening eyelashes. "What?" she whispered.

"They are bullies because they are afraid."

None of that made sense to Loulou, not at all, so it didn't help. She had only just added these girls from school to her very first Facebook page and she thought it meant they were all good friends. So, whatever was there to be afraid of? And why would that make them mean and nasty?

She just shrugged.

"Whatever," she said, quietly. Nothing made much sense now. She tried not to care. But in her heart, she did care. She cared very much about how badly it all hurt her.

"I am going to go down to the school tomorrow," Mom said, angrily. And that was that. A decision had been made. Mom would go see the head teacher and sort it all out.

5
A New Day

*N*ext morning, Loulou dressed in her school uniform just the same as usual. She walked slowly to the front door with her school bag over her shoulder. Her little legs and feet were all moving in the right direction for school, but she felt as if her brain and her heart were still tucked up in bed, wanting to hide away under the covers so nobody could get to her.

If her brain and her heart stayed at home in bed, in the comfort of her own purple bedroom, no nasty girls would be able to reach her. She smiled a little at the thought—but a bigger smile just wouldn't come.

You see, the truth was, it had been just the same at the last school; she had always been good to everyone, always tried to mind her own business and always worked hard to be the best, best friend she could to all the girls—even the ones who didn't deserve it because they were mean or cruel to others. And now, look where all that had got her. At another new school, with all the same happening all over again. Where would it end?

She reached up and stretched out her arms to encourage her mother to bend down for a kiss goodbye, the same as on any other day. But of course, Loulou had quite forgotten that today was *not* just any other day. Today was the day Mom was coming to school with her, to see the head teacher about all the nasty comments on Facebook and to see whether the head teacher would talk to them all.

Daddy had gone off to work already, but he had kissed Loulou on the top of her head and said, "Loulou, keep on being who you are, my bright, shining star. Don't let anyone get to you, baby girl."

Normally, Loulou hated being called *baby girl,* but today, it was just what she had needed to hear.

And now, instead of giving her daughter a kiss goodbye, Loulou's mom reached out her right hand to take hold of Loulou's. "C'mon little lady," she said, "Into the lions' den we go!"

Loulou loved lions so she wasn't at all sure if Mom had that bit right. School was nothing like a place where the fuzzy lions lived, she was sure of that!

But never mind; with her hand inside her mother's, she would go anywhere and feel on top of the world.

Together, they walked to the school. Mom sang happy songs on the way, hoping to stop some of Loulou's trembling. It worked and when they reached the school gate, she was even skipping a little bit.

"Mom?" she said, looking up.

"Yes, sweetpea?"

"I'm glad you're here," she said.

And with that, they went in through the big double doors of the school. Its familiar smell of chalkboards and cleaning products, of science classes for the older kids and of the old and musty gym floor reached their nostrils. Nowhere else on this earth smelled the same as school.

6
Facing the Truth

*L*oulou's mom had phoned ahead and asked if she could meet with the head teacher this morning, without saying why that was. The answer had been yes, of course she could.

Mrs. Blount was actually very nice. She had been the head teacher for five years now, replacing a woman called Mrs. Kelloff, a teacher all the girls called Mrs. Telloff, for obvious reasons.

Mrs. Blount, on the other hand, was a woman like any girl's best grandma, with round curves and big hair swept up into a bun, and with a wide smile even when a girl was mean or naughty.

Mrs. Blount believed in *loving the girls into submission*, as she put it. She made them good by not being mean; everyone liked to impress Mrs. Blount and to stay in her good books, because—among other things—Mrs. Blount gave out prizes for all sorts of good and helpful behaviour!

And who wouldn't want to win a prize? Even the school truants—the kids who dodged school given half a chance—wanted to win prizes, because she even reached into her own purse one time and pulled out a crispy $10 note for the best-behaved child in a particular class! And on another occasion, she had given one boy a half day off school to go and hunt bugs in the playground, just because the boy said he loved to hunt bugs!

She was that kind of teacher, was Mrs. Blount. Every kid loved her, even those naughty, horrid little boys who used to get sent home all the time when Mrs. Kelloff had been at the school. Mrs. Blount was always on the lookout for what she called *talent,* for kids who surprised her in a good way.

Now and then, she would bounce her way into a classroom of a morning, calling, "And where is the talent today?"

Lots of hands would shoot high into the air, even from the bad kids. By the day's end, many of them had found at least one way to do something good. And at the end of every day, every pupil filled in a little slip of paper and pushed it into the wall-mounted Talent Box in every classroom. Each paper would have only two written lines: the name of the pupil, and one very good thing they had done on that day. This had worked miracles with all the kids.

Then, at the very end of the day and just before home time, Mrs. Blount would go into each classroom and hand the teacher a certificate to give to the child who had won the day's prize. The teacher would read out who had won, and all the children would clap and cheer. Nobody was even jealous, because this happened so often that every child had a chance to be a winner.

So, Mrs. Blount would surely be very upset to hear how some of her young talents had been bullying another girl. But she had to be told.

7

Away with the Fairies

*L*oulou's mom clutched Loulou's hand very tightly while she used her other hand to *knock-knock* at Mrs. Blount's big brown door.

"Enter!" called a voice in a happy, sing-song tone. Mrs. Blount was always a joy to deal with, right from the very beginning. Her cheery tone could get rid of any doom and gloom a parent might feel.

Loulou entered first, Mom's hands resting now on both her shoulders as she steered her into the head teacher's room.

"Oh! My dear," Mrs. Blount said. "And Mom, how lovely to see you both."

All their tensions slipped away. Mrs. Blount's chubby pink face was round and squishy; if she had been a puppy, you would just want to grab those little cheeks and give them a squidgy squeeze.

"Have a seat!" she called. "Now, the most important thing first. Anyone for a nice lemonade?"

This was one of the strange but nice things about this head teacher. Even the naughty boys and girls would be asked if they wanted lemonade, and what made it even better was that Mrs. Blount made it all herself, at home, stuffing oodles and oodles of love and faith in the kids into each bottle, bringing it in to school in big glass jars.

To be given it as a good girl, well, you just felt special. But for those who were given it when they were naughty—it just confused their little minds and made them sad they had been so wicked when this lady could still be so nice to them.

Whoever heard of receiving a treat when you'd been naughty, and who could possibly be wicked in front of Mrs. Blount? It was very odd indeed. But it worked.

Both Mom and Loulou nodded their heads and received a tall glass of the magic yellow potion to calm their jangled nerves. Loulou's elbow poked Mom in the ribs just the once, as if to say, *go on, tell her why we've come.*

Mom put her daughter's laptop on the desk that stood between herself and the head teacher, opening it to Loulou's Facebook page. Then she told Mrs. Blount all about how upset Loulou had been, showing the teacher the nasty and cruel comments. To be quite honest, even she and Daddy were upset; they had never thought of themselves as poor, and Daddy had always thought he did a good job of hiding his shiny bald head under the combed-over locks of his silvery-gray hair. Nasty Facebook comments could hurt even grown-ups, though they tried not to show it.

Mrs. Blount leaned in, her eyeglasses perched on the tip of her nose as she squinted at the screen. "Oh, my," she said. "Oh, my."

Loulou pointed out with a shaky hand all the worst comments, wondering how the *oh, my* would resolve anything. She waited.

"Oh, my, my," the teacher said again, as if words failed her. Her lips opened and closed, and her jaw even seemed to tremble just a little.

"Mrs. Blount?" said Mom, wondering if she needed to slap the teacher on the back if she was choking on her own words. But the head teacher's mouth opened again, and this time, a few more words popped out.

"Well, I never did."

Loulou and Mom began to smile. This was really quite funny. Or, it would be if the situation didn't feel so utterly horrible.

"So, what do you think we should do?" Mom asked, finally.

"Do?" asked Mrs. Blount. "What do you mean, *do*? The answer is obvious, I'm sure."

Mom and Loulou looked at each other, confused. The answer was…obvious? So obvious they couldn't see it? Not even with eyeglasses on? Loulou wore her best purple reading glasses while Mom fumbled in her purse for her own pair.

"I… I'm not sure I understand," Mom said.

Mrs. Blount rose and gazed out of the window at the houses across the way, the little homes that poked their pointy roofs above the treetops.

"You see these, Mrs. Finch?"

Finch was Loulou's surname and so her mother was *Mrs. Finch*.

The head teacher's aging finger pointed toward the houses she could spot over the fields from the school.

Both Mom and Loulou nodded, not sure where this was heading.

"Well, inside all these little houses are children just like you, Loulou. You see, *all* children are good. Yes, every single one of you, even the bad ones."

Loulou scrunched up her face, still not getting what the lady was going on about. How could the bad kids be good?

As nice as she was, sometimes, Mrs. Blount seemed to be *away with the fairies*.

8

Monsters

*I*n all these houses where all the good children live," Mrs. Blount said, "are parents and siblings, care-takers and family friends. And they all have a mountain of problems. You see?"

"I…um…see," Mom said. Loulou's head nodded, hesitant. What did problems have to do with how mean these girls had been to her daughter?

"And in each of those houses with all the good children and all their relatives and family friends, and all their problems, are *monsters*."

"Monsters?" Mom exclaimed, thinking Mrs. Blount had really lost the plot now.

"Facebook monsters," the head teacher said, as if it was obvious. "Facebook monsters, my dears. You see, sometimes, the good children's lives are filled with bad things. Bad things or bad people from dawn till dusk. And the bad things make them hurt, and scared, and angry, and mean, because they don't know what else to do with their fears. And then they go on Facebook and bash it all out on their keyboards! They are not bad children; they are chasing off monsters. That, my lovely Loulou, is all Facebook—that awful place—is good for: monster-bashing!"

She laughed aloud and poured more lemonade into empty glasses.

Mom nodded; that was kind of what she'd meant when she said the kids who did this were all afraid. But Mrs. Blount put it all so wonderfully.

"Really?" Loulou asked, suddenly finding her own voice. She honestly could not imagine houses filled with top to bottom with monsters because her own home was so wonderful, and so warm and kind and filled top to bottom with love. In fact, there was so much love packed inside Loulou's home that she often wondered how they ever managed to shut the doors and windows for all the love bursting at the seams!

"Come here," Mrs. Blount said, patting a chair at her side as she looked at Loulou. The teacher turned the laptop around while Loulou sat beside her on the chair.

"Here's Lindy," said Mrs. Blount. "She's one of the little horrors who wrote the nasty comment about your father's hair."

Loulou nodded while Mom sat wide-eyed, just listening and watching.

"You know what happened to Lindy's father's hair?" she asked.

Loulou shook her head.

"Lindy's father's hair waved bye-bye. He was very sick, you see, with a disease called cancer. And he had to have a very nasty treatment, so he lost all of his thick black hair. I think Lindy is really quite jealous of your father and of how your father is still well enough to take you on a special day out."

Loulou couldn't believe her ears. Goodness, how hard that must have been for Lindy and her dad! She wanted to cry for Lindy and her dad.

"And look at Alice," the head teacher went on. "See how she made a cruel joke about your family not having very much money?"

Again, Loulou nodded, her eyes as big as gobstoppers as she wondered what would come next.

"Please never tell a soul this," she went on, "because I really should not tell you. But Alice does not have a home at all. When her mommy and daddy fell behind with their house payments, the bank took the house back. And now they live in a cheap motel, all crammed into one room. In fact, the school provides Alice's uniform because there is just no way they can afford to buy one. Alice's gym skirt is falling to pieces."

Loulou was shocked and felt so sad for Alice. Her own closet was full of nice clothes and school uniforms she didn't even wear anymore. As soon as one item got just a bit of wear, Mom went to the store and bought her a new one.

And finally, the head teacher pointed to a third photo on Loulou's Facebook page, picking out the one with her father in the *cheap* family car.

"You won't believe this, now, Loulou," Mrs. Blount said. "This super black sedan that Raheleh claims father owns, is not his car. This is a protection vehicle. Do you know what that means?"

Loulou and Mom both shook their heads.

"See the blacked-out windows?"

They nodded vigorously.

"Well, the truth is, Raheleh and her family are refugees; they fled another country because Raheleh's father is a diplomat—like, a high-ranking official—and the whole family had to run for their lives after a bad group took over their home country. They are not safe anywhere in the world. They have to be in that car everywhere they go, so Raheleh could never go to the beach like you did, not with her father, anyway. She must have been very sad to see your freedom."

A small tear dripped from Loulou's eye. She just couldn't believe what she was hearing.

She simply couldn't imagine not managing to have her freedom, having to go everywhere in a big black car with tinted windows, with adults at her side all the time, for years and years.

"So, Raheleh has probably never seen crabs or rock pools, or candy stores down by the beach, or a beach café selling fresh lemonade. So, it's a very good thing I make the lemonade for her, isn't it?" said Mrs. Blount.

Loulou and her mom felt suddenly very fortunate. Oh! These poor girls! No wonder they had turned into Facebook monsters, just like the head teacher said.

"And you asked what you could do about it?" Mrs. Blount asked. "What you *do* about it is, you be as nice as you can to these bullies, because Facebook is not the real world. This, where we are standing now, and the world I have told you about, is the real one. So, what do *Likes* and hearts and emojis matter, when some girls have no home, or are chased and threatened in their daily lives, or when their fathers are so sick that all their hair drops out?"

Loulou hung her head for thinking about all the *Likes* she had wanted to receive. Now, she hated Facebook and its pettiness, and how it made some people show off and how that turned good girls into monsters.

The truth was clear now; Facebook *Likes* really didn't matter at all—not to her, anyway—because her biggest fans were her mom and dad who were always there for her, always loving and supportive, always cheering her on.

And she remembered too, she had real friends, ones she played with, ones she'd met in the neighbourhood—and who also didn't much care for *Fakebook*, as they called it. These were kids from happy homes who liked to be outside playing.

Sure, they had Facebook accounts too, but they didn't live on their phones.

* * *

That night after brushing her teeth, Loulou signed onto her Facebook page again. Now, she could look at all the mean comments and see the other side of what they all meant. And now, she found nothing hurt her anymore.

She picked out the same mean posts her head teacher had highlighted.

First, she clicked on the comment made by Lindy, about how Loulou's father's hair would blow away.

"Too right!" she wrote, smiling, "That's funny! My dad thinks no one can see it's a comb-over! To be honest, everyone knows bald looks better." Loulou knew her father wouldn't mind.

Then she picked out Raheleh's post about the family's black sedan. "That's a super-cool car," she wrote. "Wow! That's a dream machine!"

And finally, she picked out Alice's post about Loulou's family being so poor, remembering how Mrs. Blount had said Alice did not have many clothes. She simply put a single pink heart emoji under Alice's post and ignored how very mean it had been to her. That gesture was sure to get poor Alice all in a mix-up! She smiled at the thought.

Later, Loulou wandered down into the kitchen and presented her mom with a huge bag of her very nicest clothes. "These are for Alice," she said. Her mom's eyes filled with tears and she just nodded.

"I'll take them down to the school in the morning," she said. "Mrs. Blount can pass them on, then nobody needs to know they came from us."

And that night, Loulou counted up all her blessings and was sure she reached at least three trillion! And each blessing was worth at least a hundred thousand Facebook Likes. So, who even cared about Facebook anymore?

This was the real world, and as the saying went:

If life gives you lemons, make lemonade.

She laughed and thought of Mrs. Blount and the wonderful lady's chubby cheeks.

Mrs. Blount deserved all the *Likes* in the world.

And a super big fat *emokee*. Lol.

Summary

Friendly Monsters: Behind the Computer is a poignant story that was written for the 21st-century child. In a world of smartphones, digital relationships and "viral media", it is more important than ever to highlight the dark underbelly of addiction to social media.

Using relatable characters and a spell-binding plot, this story explores how addiction to validation from others in form of digital likes and comments can rob young children and teenagers, and indeed, adults too, of their self-esteem and agency.

This little book will gradually open your children's eye to the dark side of social media to teach children the disapproval from their social media friends is not important as the approval from themselves.

C. PIERRE-RUSSELL

was born and raised in sunny Miami, FL, it was natural for Cheurlie Pierre-Russell to join the United States Navy.

Her high point came during Operation Uphold Democracy on the island nation of Haiti, where she worked as a translator. Leaving the Navy was difficult but it was time to start a family and tackle a new career.

C. Pierre-Russell graduated from Georgia State University with a Bachelor of Arts in Sociology, later earning a Master of Science in Psychology from Walden University.

Her desire to strive in education led her to study the development and perception of children's lives through the influence of social context, and she has also studied children's intellectual development.

These combined areas of interest influenced her to write children's books, to help them understand their own cognitive way of life.

A strong role model for women and children, C. Pierre-Russell is a wife and has three amazing children of her own.

Now, she writes both fiction and non-fiction for kids of all ages, covering many subjects.

C. Pierre-Russell feels every child is a future leader and deserves only the best!

To find out about C. Pierre-Russell's next book release, visit her Instagram page: https://www.instagram.com/j3russellbook/ *or her Facebook page:* https://www.facebook.com/